disc

TANA HOBAN

Of Colors and Things

A Mulberry Paperback Book

NEW YORK

This one is for Sophie and Sylvie

**The photographs were reproduced from 35mm slides
and printed in full-color.**
Copyright © 1989 by Tana Hoban.
**All rights reserved. No part of this book may be
reproduced or utilized in any form or by any means,
electronic or mechanical, including photocopying,
recording, or by any information storage or retrieval
system, without permission in writing from the
Publisher. Inquiries should be addressed to
Greenwillow Books, a division of William Morrow &
Company, Inc., 10 East 53rd Street, New York, NY 10022.**
Manufactured in China

**The Library of Congress has cataloged the
Greenwillow Books edition of**
Of Colors and Things **as follows:**
Hoban, Tana
Of colors and things/by Tana Hoban
p. cm.
**Summary: Photographs of toys, food, and other
common objects are grouped on each page
according to color.**
ISBN 0-688-07534-7. ISBN 0-688-07535-5 (lib. bdg.)
1. Color—Photographs—Juvenile literature.
[1. Color.] I. Title.
QC495.5.H62 1989
535.6—dc19 88-11101 CIP AC

09 10 11 12 13 SCP 10 9 8
First Mulberry Edition, 1996
ISBN 0-688-04585-5

duck

balloon

Flowers

candy

pumpkin

orange Juice

oranges

bib

block

pot

ribbon

toy

Mouse

elephant

tea pot

towels

bike

colored pencil

apple

cups and pitcher

corn

basket